Poppy
the Pirate Dog
and the
Treasure Keeper

Poppy the Pirate Dog and the Treasure Keeper

Liz Kessler

Illustrated by Mike Phillips

Orion
Children's Books

First published in Great Britain in 2014
by Orion Children's Books
a division of the Orion Publishing Group Ltd
Orion House
5 Upper St Martin's Lane
London WC2H 9EA
An Hachette UK Company

1 3 5 7 9 10 8 6 4 2

Text © Liz Kessler 2014
Illustrations copyright © Mike Phillips 2014

A catalogue record for this book is available from the British Library

ISBN 978 1 4440 0377 2

Printed in China

www.orionbooks.co.uk

*This book is dedicated
to the original 'Missy',
Miss Havisham*

Contents

Chapter One	11
Chapter Two	25
Chapter Three	35
Chapter Four	43
Chapter Five	51
Chapter Six	67

Chapter One

Poppy the Pirate Dog was out on the high seas with her shipmates.

It was Mum's birthday tomorrow and Tim and Suzy were putting on a pirate show to celebrate.

First, they built a ship.

Then they raised the sails.

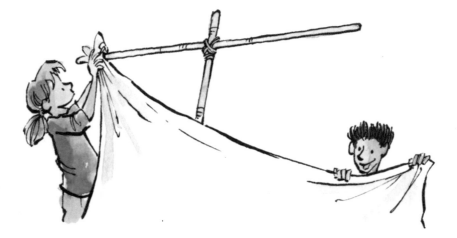

George was hunting for treasure.

And Poppy had the best job ever –
she was the Treasure Keeper.

The Treasure Keeper is a very
important member of a pirate crew.

They are good at hiding things.

They are so fierce that no one will
dare try to steal their treasure.

And most of all, they're brilliant at staying in one place and guarding the treasure at all times.

'Come on, crew,' Tim said, as
George came back to the boat with a
new piece of treasure. 'We need to get
everything ship-shape. Mum's going to
have the best birthday ever!'

Poppy studied the treasure George had brought. Where could she hide this one?

Inside the safe?

On the roof?

Maybe she should just stay still and guard it.

Being a Treasure Keeper wasn't easy.

'Ahoy there!' Suzy called.

'Suzy!' It was Mum. 'I hope that isn't my best pink sheet you're using.'

'Oops,' said Suzy, lowering the sail and jumping ship. 'Back in a minute.'

'Ahoy there!' called Tim.

'Tim! Have you got my stepladder?' called Dad.

'Oops,' said Tim.

Dad helped Tim take down the ship's front deck. 'And don't forget about Mum's birthday,' Dad said.

'Of course we haven't forgotten,' Suzy said. 'We're putting on a special show!'

'What have you bought her?' Tim asked Dad.

Dad smiled. 'The prettiest, sparkliest, twinkliest necklace in the world. She's going to love it.'

And off he went with the stepladder.

Chapter Two

Poppy was trying hard to be the best Treasure Keeper ever. She gathered the treasure and went to look for some new hiding places.

But she had so much treasure in
her mouth, she couldn't see where she
was going.

Poppy wobbled this way and that, and before you could say, 'Yo, ho, ho and a bottle of rum,' she had crashed into Tim and fallen overboard.

Treasure spilled everywhere.

No one noticed something shiny
and twinkly fly out from inside some
crinkly paper and land on a big,
round rock.

'Poppy!' Suzy cried, running down the garden. 'Are you OK?'

It's my eye, Poppy thought. I think I've broken it. Not only was she a rubbish Treasure Keeper, now she couldn't even see out of both eyes.

'She's got a cut on her eye,'
Tim said.

Poppy curled into Suzy's arms.
All pirates need a hug sometimes.

'Come on, Poppy,' Tim said, stroking Poppy's face. 'We need to get you to the vet.'

The vet? The man who prodded and poked her and sometimes stuck needles in her leg? She wasn't going *there*! Her eye was fine. It didn't hurt much at all. She tried to open it. Ouch!

'Wait,' Tim said. 'I've got an idea.'
He ran into the house and came back
with some pirate books.

Poppy rested her head on Tim's leg
and looked at the pictures, with her
good eye.

'Do you see?' Tim said. He was pointing at a pirate surrounded by shiny gold treasure. 'That one's the Treasure Keeper. And look at his face! All the best Treasure Keepers wear eye patches. You'll be just like them.'

Poppy studied the picture. Tim was right! She hoped they could see the vet soon. She was going to be the best pirate dog in the world.

Chapter Three

Poppy sulked all the way home from the vet's. She wasn't the best pirate dog in the world. And she wasn't wearing an eye patch.

She was wearing an enormous,
see-through, plastic collar around
her neck.

It looked a bit like the lampshade
in the living room.

Poppy had never felt *less* like a
pirate.

She went straight to her bed. She
didn't even get up when the doorbell
rang. She just lay there feeling
miserable.

Tim and Suzy opened the door. It was the next-door neighbours, Mr and Mrs Roy, with their son, Kieran.

'Sorry to bother you,' Mrs Roy said. 'We wondered if you'd seen our baby tortoise, Missy? We haven't seen her since yesterday.'

Tim and Suzy shook their heads.

'Sorry,' Suzy said.

'But we'll keep a look-out,' Tim added.

'Oh, thank you,' Mr Roy said.

As they turned to leave, Poppy noticed Kieran glance over. He was staring right at Poppy.

What are you looking at? Poppy thought grumpily.

Kieran burst out laughing. 'I thought you said she was a pirate dog,' he said. 'I didn't know pirates wore giant ice-cream cones on their heads!'

It's a lampshade, actually, thought
Poppy, as she got up and marched into
the garden.

Chapter Four

Poppy lay in a patch of sunlight near the pirate ship. Of *course* she was a pirate dog. No wonder that boy's pet tortoise had run away if he was so horrible all the time.

Poppy tried to get comfy, but each time she moved, the sunlight shone on her plastic collar.

She moved again and a ray of sun
hit something on the grass. Something
pretty and sparkly and twinkly.

What was it?

The thing twinkled again.

Was it... Could it be . . . ?

Pirate treasure?

The treasure was tangled on a big round rock. Who needed a silly eye patch anyway? This was her chance to prove she was the best Treasure Keeper ever.

Poppy tugged at the treasure with her teeth. It didn't budge.

Oh well. All she had to do was stand
here, next to the treasure, and guard it
with her life. Just wait till Tim and Suzy
saw her!

A moment later, she jumped in fright. Because the big round rock suddenly did something that big round rocks don't usually do.

It sprouted legs and moved.

Poppy ran into the house and hid under the kitchen table. Maybe I'm not cut out to be a Treasure Keeper after all, she thought.

Chapter Five

Next morning, Poppy decided to go and find her pirate treasure. I'm Poppy the Pirate Dog, she thought. I'm not scared of a walking rock.

Suzy and Tim were helping Dad make breakfast.

'What did Mum think of her birthday present?' Suzy asked.

'She doesn't think anything yet,' Dad said. 'I can't believe I've lost it. It really was the prettiest, sparkliest thing you've ever seen.'

Poppy's ears pricked up. Wait.
Pretty? Sparkly?

'I hid it under the bed,' Dad said.
'It was wrapped in lovely crinkly paper
covered in orange flowers and red
hearts. But I can't find it anywhere.'

Poppy didn't know anything about orange flowers and red hearts, but there was definitely something pretty and sparkly outside on the walking rock. Could it be Mum's birthday present?

Dad sighed. 'I'll just have to hope breakfast in bed will be a nice enough birthday treat.'

As Dad went upstairs, Suzy got up from the table. 'Come on, Tim, let's help Dad look for Mum's present. It's got to be in the house somewhere.'

Poppy thought about how the treasure yesterday had sparkled in the sunlight. Suddenly she knew for sure what it was.

She ran to the table and nudged Tim.

Tim stroked her head as he got up from the table. 'Can't play now, Poppy,' he said.

Poppy ran to Suzy.

'Later, Poppy,' Suzy said. 'We're busy.'

Poppy went to the back door and whined. Come on, come on. There's no time to waste.

'Later, Poppy!' Suzy said firmly.

No! Not later! Now! Poppy whined louder.

Tim sighed. 'Oh, OK. We'll play for five minutes,' he said. 'Then we've got to look for the necklace.'

Finally! thought Poppy, as Suzy
and Tim followed her into the garden.

Poppy looked around. Where had it gone?

'There's nothing here,' Suzy said.
'Nothing except that rock.'

Yes! It was still there! Poppy moved
her head to make the light bounce on
her plastic collar. It shone right onto
the rock.

The treasure twinkled.

The rock stuck out a leg.

Poppy barked.

Suzy squealed.

'Mum's necklace!' Tim yelled.

'You found it!'

Suzy knelt down and reached
carefully for the necklace. 'That's not
all she's found,' she said. She picked
up the rock and untangled the treasure
from around its legs.

Tim grinned. 'Poppy, you found
Missy!' he said. 'You're the best.'

'The very best pirate dog in the world,' Suzy added.

Poppy wagged her tail. I am, aren't I? she thought.

Chapter Six

That afternoon, Poppy the Pirate Dog
and her crew performed their special
pirate birthday show for Mum.

The Roys had been so happy to find Missy the tortoise that they said she could be part of the crew as well – as long as they could come and watch the show.

Kieran even brought Poppy a bone
to say sorry for being mean.

Tim steered the pirate ship.

Suzy raised the brand new sails.

George guarded the deck while
Poppy kept a look-out.

And Missy? Well, they had the
perfect job for her.

A job that could only *really* be done by someone who knew how to stay still and guard things.

Missy was the Treasure Keeper and she was making sure that none of the treasure went missing.

As the show came to an end and the audience stood up and cheered, Poppy looked round at her shipmates and felt proud.

Maybe the best job isn't Treasure Keeper, she thought. Maybe it's Treasure *Finder*. And maybe the best pirates don't wear patches on their eyes. Maybe the super-*super*-special pirates wear lampshades around their necks.

What are you going to read next?

Have more adventures with Horrid Henry,

and travel the world with Miranda the Explorer.

Play clever tricks with Twit,

spend Mondays at Monster School,

and even brave The Dragon's Dentist . . .

Learn how love is just like a Woolly Hat,

dance under The Little Nut Tree,

take home Monstar, the best pet ever,

and have an extra-special Mr Monkey birthday party!

Enjoy all the Early Readers.